My Bed is an Air Balloon

Julia Copus & Alison Jay

ff

FABER & FABER

When night falls my bed is an air balloon.

I sail through the slipsiverse, close by the moon.

I float above treetops where fluttertufts are sleeping

And flowering hills where the whifflepigs go creeping;

Ponds strung with starlight that glitter like glass,

A floog with her velvet nose bent to the grass.

Such treasures I spy on! My bed in the trees

Swings me up high, like a circus trapeze.

Now the cool, night-rustling air

Slips through my finger-gaps, ripples my hair;

Now we glide over water, the moon's silver light

Blown by a cloudpuff into the bight,

Adrift on the sea where the dream-shapes float;

When night falls my bed is a sailing boat.

When night falls my bed is a sailing boat

Adrift on the sea where the
dream-shapes float,

Blown by a cloudpuff into the bight.

Now we glide over water; the moon's silver light

Slips through my finger-gaps, ripples my hair;

Now the cool, night-rustling air

Swings me up high, like a circus trapeze.

Such treasures I spy on my bed in the trees –

A floog with her velvet nose bent to the grass,

Ponds strung with starlight that glitter like glass

And flowering hills where the whifflepigs go creeping.

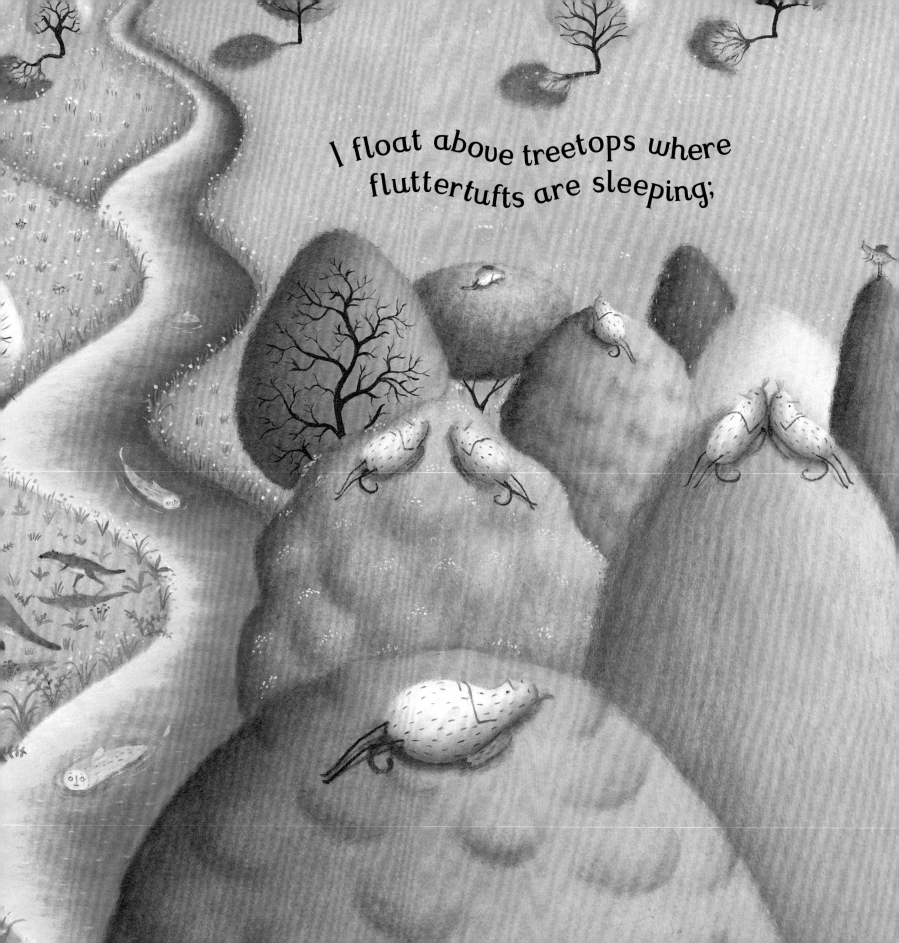

I float above treetops where
fluttertufts are sleeping;

I sail through the slipsiverse, close by the moon.

↠ A FABER PICTURE BOOK ↞

My Bed is an Air Balloon

Julia Copus & Alison Jay

First published in the UK in 2018 · First published in the US in 2018
by Faber and Faber Limited, Bloomsbury House, 74-77 Great Russell Street London, WC1B 3DA

Designed by Faber and Faber
Printed in China

Text © Julia Copus, 2018 · Illustrations © Alison Jay, 2018

A CIP record for this book is available from the British Library

HB ISBN 978-0-571-33484-1 · PB ISBN 978-0-571-34771-1

2 4 6 8 10 9 7 5 3 1

When night falls my bed
is an air balloon.